MW00772722

THE LEGACY *of* TALBOT HALL

a novel

PATTI BAUMHOWER

"The Legacy of Talbot Hall"
by Patti Baumhower

TATE PUBLISHING *& Enterprises*

TATE PUBLISHING
& Enterprises

The Legacy of Talbot Hall
Copyright © 2006 by Patti Baumhower. All rights reserved.

No part of this publication may be reproduced, stored in a retrieval system or transmitted in any way by any means, electronic, mechanical, photocopy, recording or otherwise without the prior permission of the author except as provided by USA copyright law.

This novel is a work of fiction. However, several names, descriptions, entities and incidents included in the story are based on the lives of real people.

Book design copyright © 2006 by Tate Publishing, LLC. All rights reserved.
Cover design by "Taylor Rauschkolb"
Interior design by "Rusty Eldred"

Published in the United States of America

ISBN: 1-5988660-4-4
06.02.10

The Legacy of Talbot Hall is a fictional story laced with true historical events.

It is a story of a family fiercely dedicated to preserving their family heritage. How the fears, joys, disappointments and successes of each generation affects the next. A story that is enjoyable for all. The author's Southern roots are reflective in the grammar and humor of the story.

I would hope that the reader after reading the Talbot's story would reflect on their heritage and have a desire to search their roots.

"We are who we are, because they were."

Patti Baumhower

DEDICATED TO:

My aunt, Willo Mae Davenport, for a lifetime of love and unquestioning support.

My husband, Bob, for his untiring "editing."

My children, Bobby, (Leslie), Debbie, KK, (John), David, Skip and (Poonam) for their enthusiastic encouragement in the writing of Talbot Hall. Especially Skip... for his sometimes not so gentle pushing to finish the Talbot's story.

My Grandchildren; Evan, Adam, John Robert, Tommy, Joshua, Spencer, Jessica, Katelynn, Anne Kathrine, Alexandra, Wesley, Yasmeen and my great, John Michael.

Especially Evan and Adam. It was their endless requests for Nana's stories that gave birth to this one.

THE LEGACY *of* TALBOT HALL

The Beginning

CHAPTER 1

Jeremiah Joseph Talbot is an energetic, ambitious 16 (soon to be 17) year old young man, who loves living in the modern, bustling town of Edenton, North Carolina.

It is 1775.

Most of his spare time you can find him by the docks, listening to the tales of the seaman as they try to out do one another with their adventurous tales of travels on the seas. The tall masts, the sails, the lines of the ships are visions of beauty to him.

He enjoys sitting by the open window of his bedroom at night breathing in the smell of the water, watching the ships anchored in the moonlight and listening to the moans they make. He knows they long to be free with their sails full, headed for mysterious places. He would close his eyes and let his imagination take him away on them.

Only thirteen more days and his Uncle Joseph will be here! How he looks forward to his visits. Uncle Joseph is his father Samuel's older (and only) brother and is like a second Father to him. He comes for visits about twice, sometimes three times a year, always bringing wonderful gifts for his mother, father and himself.

His Father and Uncle Joseph look close enough alike to be twins. Both tall, black hair, blue eyes, large muscular build. Uncle Joseph laughs loud and often jokes, dresses flamboyantly and is generous with his affection.

He loves listening to stories about all the places his Uncles travels have taken him. He has been to France, England, Asia, Africa, Egypt, India and wherever else his business or adventurous spirit takes him. He has no children of his own and dotes on Jeremiah.

His father, Samuel Jeremiah, is an expert craftsman in design and building. He is described as a very kind but serious, intent man. The only time he willingly dresses up is for church service at Saint Paul's on Sundays. He gives the best hugs and when he smiles, his whole face glows.

Being the perfectionist at his craft that he is, his reputation is well known far beyond Chowan County and there is always a waiting for his craft.

The building of the magnificent new courthouse demands his expertise in design and his superbly crafted furniture. He works long hours to keep up with those demands and those of his regular customers, most often with Jeremiah as one of his apprentice. Being intent there is very little conversation between them while they work, other than instructions.

He really did not mind. When they left work, he again was his Father and they could talk about everything. They hunted and fished often. When he was six, his Father made him a little red pull cart that was the envy of all his friends. Four years ago for his birthday, he made his bedroom look like a ship captain's quarters.

Such wonderful times would be filed away in his memory

to be pulled up and dwelled on many times in the future. Summer evenings would usually find the Talbot's on the front porch of their home.

It faced the bay and the soft breeze off the water, fragrance from his mother's garden, the creak of the chairs as they slowly rocked and the distant bell from the ships anchored in the harbor were "heavens medicine" his mother would say, almost every night.

He thought his Mother was the most wonderful woman God had ever created.

Maureen O'Malley Talbot.

He had his mother's auburn curly hair and green eyes. She wore her hair swooped up on top of her head but there were always curly wisps around her face and neck. She always fussed about it but Samuel said it made her look like the angel she was.

She was always taking her famous baked goods or flowers from her flower filled yard to friends and even those she barely knew, when they needed cheering up. Often there would be people standing by their house admiring his mother's garden. Flowers of every color you could imagine. And the smells that floated from her kitchen seemed to lift you up and pull you in. She was magic in the kitchen. Each year that Maureen entered her cakes and jams in the county fair, the others felt they might as well concede. (And they were right)!

She believed you should apologize when you are wrong but when you are right, stand strong. Samuel and Jeremiah were not surprised when just the year before she joined forty-nine other ladies and protested the "outrageous tax laws!" England was attaching. They vowed not to drink any more tea or to wear cloth from Britain in protest. Her green eyes flashed that day as she told them how she felt compelled to stand with the other ladies in protest. "Wrong is wrong! I shall do my part!" They watched astonished as she ceremoniously spread her favorite tea among her flowers.

Jeremiah could see the admiration in his Fathers eyes.

"Jeremiah, are you picking those flowers for Mrs. Ambrose or a certain young lady on Main Street?" Maureen jokingly asked. She really didn't need a reply. She knew they were for Jane.

Jeremiah had known Jane all of his life. Their families shared a pew at Saint Paul's. She had always been in his life. He couldn't imagine life without her. They had played together, schooled together and being sweet on each other just seemed to come natural.

To Jeremiah she was a vision of beauty, with hair as black as a raven and eyes a violet color that he had only seen in his Mothers' garden. She moved and spoke softly. The perfect lady. His lady.

He finished the bouquet, called his dog Hungry, poked his head in the kitchen door and told his Mother that he would be back at dinnertime.

Jane was in the back yard swing when he arrived. Ever present Darlin was with her. Darlin's Mother, Cinnamon, was the Sullivan's house servant. Darlin was born one week before Jane and they had always been together. Darlin's name was really Darlene, but Jane pronounced it as Darlin when she started to talk, and now everyone called her Darlin.

When it came to Jane, Darlin could be less than darling. She was very protective of her. Jane had a frail childhood and Mr. Sullivan had instructed Darlin at a very early age to look out for her. And that she did!

Jane and Jeremiah sat in the swing, drinking lemonade, lost in conversation until Darlin said, "Mr. Jeremiah you best go home. There is a mighty black cloud above and that wind is acting up."

She was right. It had been cloudy, rainy and windy for a couple of days, but this was *much* worse. He said his goodbyes, called Hungry and started the four blocks to his home. The wind was very strong and getting stronger, and the sky was getting blacker. It was raining hard. He grabbed Hungry up in his arms, running. He felt a little sick. He had never seen anything like this. Things were blowing all around him as he finally got to his back yard. His Father was trying to close the shop door. Jeremiah put Hungry down and helped. He saw his Mother standing by the kitchen door.

He heard her calling, "Please hurry! Come in!" They got the door secured and ran for the kitchen.

"Where is Hungry?"

"He ran behind the shop," his Mother said. Jeremiah turned and ran for the shop. The last thing he heard was his Mother's voice screaming "Jeremiah, No!"

Then everything went black.

CHAPTER 2

He seemed to float. He could hear voices in the distance and then they would fade. He would see misty shadows and then they too would fade. His head hurt. In fact he hurt all over. This dream seemed to be lasting far too long. He wished his Mother would come wake him. Why didn't she come? He heard his name being called, but it wasn't his Mother. Who was calling him? Why couldn't he see them?

"Who is it?" he asked.

"Oh, thank you sweet Jesus! He's awake!" He knew that voice. It was Cinnamon, Darlin's mother. But why is she here he wondered and why was she in his room calling him?

"Jeremiah, open your eyes, Boy!" someone said in a strong voice. He tried, but the light hurt his eyes. He lifted his arm and tried to block the light.

"Pull that drape a bit"… again from the commanding voice.

"Open your eyes I say, Boy!"

"Uncle Joseph? Is that you?"

"Yes, Boy, it is I."

His voice was suddenly tender.

Uncle Joseph was leaning over him and he could see the worried look on his face. "Are you alright, Boy?" he asked gently. "Yes, sir, I am, but that was a terrible storm yesterday. Was your ship damaged?"

Then he noticed his surroundings.

This wasn't his room.

"Where am I?"

"Why am I here?"

He felt an uneasy feeling creeping over him.

"Where are Mother and Father?"

Uncle Joseph's shoulders sagged a little and he looked down towards the floor.

"*Uncle Joseph*?" His voice was questioning and full of fear now.

Uncle Joseph spoke very softly and slowly, "Boy, you have to be brave. What I have to tell you is tragic. The storm wasn't yesterday. It was 9 days ago. We didn't know if you would pull out or not. The oak, next to the house, was blown over. It hit the backside of the house and caught all three of you. I'm sorry Boy…your Mother and Father… were killed."

He heard the words, but they were wrong! It is not true! They couldn't be gone. "Mother…Father? No! It's not so! Not so!" Sobbing, he cried until he fell asleep still in Uncle Joseph's arms.

Jeremiah remained at the Sullivan's, being cared for by Jane, Darlin, Mrs. Sullivan and Cinnamon. Uncle Joseph attended to the affairs of his brother and his sister-in-law.

The Sullivan's were more concerned about Jeremiah's behavior than his health. He was getting stronger, eating well but he was so quiet. Not his normal exuberant self. They knew he was grieving but when they spoke to him, it was as if he could not hear. He seemed to be in his own world. Jane was frantic. She did not understand what was happening to him.

"Father, he won't even talk to me. He just stares out the window. What can I do?"

"Jeremiah has had a great loss, My Dear. One that affected him very deeply. People handle grief differently. We have to be patient and give him the time he needs to accept what has happened. Just keep asking God to help him."

It was another four days before Jeremiah was able to leave the Sullivan's with Uncle Joseph. They went for a walk together.

"Boy, do want to go to your house?" asked Uncle Joseph.

"No, not yet."

Hungry walked by his side. There was a special place in his heart now for Darlin. It was she that went looking for Hungry after the storm and had cared for him. They walked in silence towards the bay.

The townspeople offered their sympathy as they passed. Everyone knew of his loss. Mr. Hewes approached Jeremiah and his uncle, removing his hat. He put his hand on Jeremiah's shoulder as he introduced himself to Uncle Joseph. "You, Dear Sir, must be the uncle of Jeremiah. I am Joseph Hewes. My pleasure to meet you, Sir."

Uncle Joseph, bowed slightly and said, "The honor is mine, Congressman."

Looking deeply into Jeremiah's eyes Mr. Hewes said, "Jeremiah, my son, I am filled with sorrow for the loss of your beloved parents. They were wonderful people. I admired them greatly. I will be home for a few days during congress recess. My dear boy, if I may be of any assistance please do not hesitate to beckon me."

Jeremiah could tell he meant every word. Jeremiah thanked him and they continued towards the bay. Knowing how much his parents respected Mr. Hewes, it meant a lot to hear him speak so kindly about them.

Reaching the bay, they sat by the waters edge in silence. The water was calm and the boats barely moved in the soft breeze.

Finally Jeremiah said, "Uncle Joseph, what will happen to me now?"

"You will return with me to Talbot Hall. I am your guardian now, Boy. I cannot take Samuel and Maureen's place, but you know I love you as my own."

He knew that.

He loved Uncle Joseph too.

CHAPTER 3

Jeremiah stood in front of his home. The fallen tree had been removed and the back of the house repaired. Uncle Joseph had seen to that. His Mothers flowers were showing their beautiful colors.

The chairs and swing his Father had made were in their places on the porch.

Everything looked normal. Why couldn't it be, he thought.

"I had some things sent ahead to Talbot Hall," Uncle Joseph was saying. "Take everything, if you want. We have the room."

Jeremiah walked into the house. The big clock was gone. The furniture from the parlor, hall table, the dish cabinet with all his Mothers dishes, was gone also. He walked upstairs into his room. It had been emptied.

Back down the stairs and into the kitchen. He picked up the biscuit jar and said "This, too." It was where his Mother kept the sweet bread.

In his parents room he picked up his Mothers treasure box. His Father had made it for her when they first married. The wood was beautifully polished and carved with exquisite flowers. Inside was a lock of Jeremiah's baby hair, his first tooth, a poem his Father had written, a letter from Maureen's Mother, a pressed flower, two pretty rocks Joseph had brought from India and the key that locked the chest.

He loved the treasure box. When he was very little his Mother had shown him the secret compartment and had let him hide things. It was a family secret she said. "No one else can ever know." He had never told anyone the secret. Not even to Jane.

His Fathers workshop was cleaned out. The damaged roof showed its new repair. Uncle Joseph stood by the door watching.

"There was a lot of water damage. Most of his drawings were destroyed. I saved what I could. His tools were ok," he said.

"Thank you. It was the courthouse drawings. It doesn't matter. They are finished building."

Outside he saw that even Hungry's house was gone. Uncle Joseph had taken care of everything.

"For awhile we will let the house. The Bateman family has offered to find suitable tenants and to watch it for you. When you are older, then you can make the decision on what to do. Two days and The Dolly Moorland will arrive."

Jeremiah again walked through his home, touching, remembering, he took a deep breath and walked out.

The next two days passed quickly. Jeremiah had said his goodbyes to friends and neighbors. There were no relatives here. Uncle Joseph was all he had now. He was leaving the only life he had known but taking his memories with him. That will have to be enough, he thought.

He asked Jane to go for a walk with him. They walked towards the bay, past the courthouse his Father had helped design and build and stopped by the huge old oak.

They could see The Dolly Moorland at anchor.

"We leave at the high tide. Uncle Joseph has made plans for me to attend school like he always said. I will be a long ways from here, Jane. *Please*, do not forget me."

Jane looked up at him, her violet eyes full of tears.

"I am so happy that you have Uncle Joseph to care for you. I will miss you dreadfully…but forget you….never!"

She took his hand, held it with hers and with her white lace handkerchief tied the two together.

"Jeremiah…just as our hands are bound…I am bound to you. I will be here when you return…waiting." Her words were embedded in his heart.

CHAPTER 4

Jeremiah stood at the stern of the ship as it left the bay and turned into the Albemarle. He breathed a prayer for God's protection on Jane and her family, turned and walked forward towards the bow, towards his future.

The Dolly Mooreland was magnificent. Joseph had a fleet of merchant ships…but this one was his pride. Jeremiah recalled the story his uncle had told him about the Dolly Moorland two years ago when he sailed the sleek craft into Edenton Bay.

People gathered at the dock just to gaze out at her setting at anchor. It seems his uncle had delivered a shipment of cargo to Bermuda and had seen the sloop docked. There were strong features of the sloop that made it so desirable to him. It was made of cedar, which made it durable and gave it rot resistance. It had a smaller hull, so it could sail into shallow waters, something larger and heavier ships could not do.

And it was fast!

Uncle Joseph had already heard stories from fellow merchants who had Bermuda Sloops that were able to save their ships and cargo because they could outrun the pirates.

When he was told the new ship was for sale he bought her on the spot and christened her, "The Dolly Moorland."

His Mother had told him Dolly Moorland was the name of the only woman he ever loved and it looked like, would be the only one. Sadly, she had been killed in a carriage accident, shortly before they were to marry.

Jeremiah stood at the bow and let the wet, salty wind hit his face. It was just as he had always imagined! The gentle sea saw of the sloop as she slid through the waves reminded him of the rocking chairs on his front porch. He looked down at Hungry by his side. Hungry didn't think much of this big, new rocking chair.

They had left Edenton Bay, entered the Albemarle Sound and were now in the Atlantic.

"Boy, look to your right. That is the island of Okracoke." Uncle Joseph informed him.

He had heard all about Okracoke from his Father. He had been there as a boy and described the island as beautiful. He had told him Blackbeard the notorious pirate had made his home there and thought it too bad, it was all people wanted to remember about the island.

One of the ship hands relieved Uncle Joseph at the steering wheel and he instructed Jeremiah in the tasks that would be his responsibility on the trip.

He eagerly listened. He wanted to learn! "How long will our trip take?" he asked.

"Two weeks or more. Depends on the weather and I do plan to make a stop at St. Augustine."

Jeremiah was trying hard to control his excitement. He was going to see sights of the world! St Augustine! Oh, how many times he and his Father discussed Castillo de San Marcos and how someday they would sail there.

"*I'll enjoy it for both of us, Father*" he thought.

"Uncle Joseph, why did you choose to live so far from us?"

"I guess you can say it chose me."

"How did that happen?'

"I made my Port in Chesapeake for years. I became acquainted with a businessman there named Leon del la Rosa. Likeable fellow. Very successful. I had many shipping contracts with him. I received an urgent beckoning from him one evening. He had a proposition for me. I was to load and ship his home and business effects to New York. There, they would be transferred to another ship for the final destination. I tried to secure that contract also, but to no avail. He said the transaction would have to be as he stated.

In exchange for a money payment, he wanted to transfer ownership of one of his holdings... a house, stable, and five hundred acres on the eastern shore of Mobile Bay."

"Had you ever seen it?"

"Well, no, not his place, but I had been in the territory on business. It was late one May afternoon when we entered into the bay. I decided to anchor out and pull into Fort Mobile early morning. Meecha brought my mug of coffee and I sat there on that hatch," he said pointing, "and watched, without doubt, the most beautiful sunset I had ever seen. I accepted the deal. I asked Del La Rosa where his final destination would be. He said he did not want to tell me. It was best I did not know."

"What did he mean?" Jeremiah asked.

His interest was peaked about this mysterious transaction.

"I asked no further. It was about a year afterwards before I finally went to the property."

"What was it like? Mother and Father always said you loved your home and that is why you lived so far away."

Uncle Joseph smiled and nodded

"I arrived early in the day. The waters were calm and the weather fair, but the place was not easy to find. From the bay there were no visible signs of life and as far as eyes could see there was nothing but sand and huge trees. I had to rely on the map he had drawn me."

Jeremiah listened intently to the mystery about what was to be his new home.

"Sighting the landmark of Ecor Rouge, we anchored the Dolly Moorland and took a skiff to shore. I found the hidden slew and stairs," Uncle Joseph continued.

"*Stairs*?" Jeremiah asked.

"Yes, the property is on a cliff and stairs were built for easy access to the top, and when I did reach the top, there was a shock."

"What? What was it?"

"Jeremiah, it looked as if your Mother had lived there. Flowers of all color lining the path that led to the house. Everything well kept."

"Well kept? After a year? Who was doing it? Did you know?"

Uncle Joseph laughed one of his infectious laughs. He loved Jeremiahs enthusiasm!

"No. I did not know. When I entered the dwelling, there was a letter on the table that explained everything."

"From who? Mr. del la Rosa?"

"Yes."

"What did it say?"

"He explained everything. Jeremiah, it seems that Mr. del la Rosa was not who he presented himself to be."

"You mean he was an imposter?"

"No. He was in fact del la Rosa but he was also known as…Carsica."

"What!" Jeremiah could not believe his ears!

"*Carsica*? Not…"

"Yes," Uncle Joseph said. "The pirate."

"You mean I will live in a pirate's house! *Carsica's* house?"

"It would seem so," Uncle Joseph said with another laugh.

"Well, who was taking care of the property?"

"He had left the caretakers for me. They take good care of everything when I am away."

From that point on the ship could not sail fast enough for Jeremiah. They stopped at St. Augustine for supplies that were needed. He watched as Meecha selected fruits, vegetables, flour and other needs, bargaining with the vendors. They were all friendly with him. They like him, Jeremiah thought. He did, too.

Meecha looked like a Grandfather with his white hair, happy eyes and just the right size lap for crawling up on to listen to great stories. Not by any means that he would! He was *way* too old for that but Meecha was just the kind of Grandfather he would want. He had never known either of his. His parents had always told him wonderful stories about them.

The famous fort amazed Jeremiah…the activity, the smells, the merchandise, the people, but when Uncle Joseph said it was time to leave…he was ready. The house was waiting.

An eager pupil, he learned a lot about ship life on the remainder of the trip. A storm they encountered gave him a quick maturity. It came upon them at night.

"A creeper," Mango, one of the hands had said. "They creep up and jump on you."

He didn't want anyone to see how scared he was, but he was trembling all over. He couldn't even talk to anyone because he was too busy praying! He wondered a few times if he would ever see his seventeenth birthday.

When the storm ended, every man on the ship was on deck, kneeling, as Uncle Joseph gave thanks to God for their safe passage. The storm had also shown him why his uncle loved this particular ship. She had proven herself to be everything his uncle had said.

He decided that someday he, too, would own a Bermuda Sloop.

The remainder of the trip seemed to pass fairly quickly. There is always steady work on a continuously sailing ship. Work, eat, and then sleep. That is the routine. Everyone worked shifts. The night watch was his favorite. He loved looking at the stars.

He would think of Jane and wonder if she was looking at the same ones. He missed her terribly already. Tonight he wondered…would she receive the shawl he had paid to be delivered to her from St. Augustine? Did she miss him?

"Watch over," a strong voice said.

He turned to see Mathias standing behind him. It had taken him awhile to get to know Mathias. He didn't have much to say, and being the straight forward man he was, if you asked him what he thought about something, you might not like his answer. Jeremiah kept his distance at first. He was a tall man, with long salt and pepper hair, no beard but the longest, strangest mustache he had ever seen. He had asked Uncle Joseph if Mathias had been a pirate, because he sure looked like one. Uncle Joseph roared with laughter.

He said Mathias was one of the gentlest, most loyal men you would ever want to know, and that is exactly what Jeremiah discovered.

It had made him think of what his Mother had always said…"Don't judge a book by its cover, Jeremiah."

I see what you mean, Mother, he thought.

The sky was breaking into a beautiful pink and blue light.

"Fair day ahead," Mathias said.

"Yes, it looks that way. Thanks, Mathias."

He went below.

"Your favorite," Meecha called to him from the galley. "Pancakes!"

"Meecha, you are my hero!"

He ate and went to bed.

CHAPTER 5

It seemed as if he had just closed his eyes when Meecha woke him from his sleep. "Captain wants you at helm."

He scurried quickly. He knew it had to be important to be awakened and summoned to the helm. Uncle Joseph saw the look on his face as he ran towards him.

He laughed saying, "Relax boy. All is well. I wanted you to have first view of Mobile Bay."

Relieved, he walked forward, stood at the bow and watched as they entered the bay. Although it was smaller it reminded him of the Albemarle.

The sloop, sail full, entered the bay.   "Uncle Joseph is right. I see nothing but trees and sand," he thought. Eventually the ship slowly turned towards the eastern shore. The anchor was lowered.

"Make ready to go ashore, Boy." Uncle Joseph said.

"Gladly, Sir!"

He gathered his belongings, found Hungry and said his goodbyes. He did not know how soon he would see the crew again. They had become his friends and he would miss them. The skiff headed towards shore. They followed the shoreline and turned towards what appeared to be a huge fallen tree. They were going to go right under the tree!

Uncle Joseph told him that even the Dolly Moorland entered the slew easily when her masts were down. He said because of fear from his *other* profession, del la Rosa had the slew deepened and hidden.

As the skiff passed smoothly under the tree, the dock and stairs appeared before his eyes.

They climbed the stairs and at the top Jeremiah had his first view of Talbot Hall. He stopped, mouth open, and said, "*Uncle Joseph!*" shocked by the grandeur of what lay before him.

"Your new home, my boy," Uncle Joseph chuckled.

The tall, red brick house stood proudly with one-floor wings to each side. The upper and lower porches extended to both sides of the two story main house; supported by thick, round, white columns. The top porch had a railing surrounding it, with glass doors opening from the upstairs rooms. Large white rocking chairs sat, quietly waiting, on both porches. Dark green shutters were mounted on each window, ready to protect from the strong winds.

They walked the curved, flower lined path towards the house. Flowers in November! It is incredible, Jeremiah thought. As they approached the house the door opened and a black woman with a huge smile emerged.

"Welcome home, Captain Talbot. And you, young sir, must be our Jeremiah. Welcome home to you, too."

I like this woman, he thought.

"Thank you, Annie." said the Captain.

"Yes, thank you, Annie." Jeremiah replied.

As they entered the house Annie said, "I have biscuits and honey ready for you. Oh, and some fresh lemonade. Come when you're ready."

She disappeared towards the back of the house.

Jeremiah and Uncle Joseph were now standing in the

foyer. Stairs curved down from the upstairs balcony walkway. There was a huge painting in a thick, gold, ornate frame on the upper balcony. It was the only painting in the room. Jeremiah couldn't take his eyes off it. Uncle Joseph walked to his side.

"Recognize the scene, Boy?" he said.

Jeremiah looked at him, then the painting.

"It looks just like my Mothers yard," he said slowly.

"Indeed it should. I had it commissioned for your Mother, but alas, the finished piece would not fit a wall in your home. She told me I should take her garden to my home and enjoy the fragrance. It has brought me much pleasure, and now it will pleasure you."

"Uncle Joseph, it is magnificent."

Just then deep, melodic clock chimes started to strike the hour. He turned and faced his parent's huge clock as it welcomed him to his new home. It was his seventeenth birthday. Wednesday, November 15, 1775.

Pointing upward, Uncle Joseph said, "That is the door to your room, Boy. Go have a look."

Jeremiah walked up the stairs, staring at the painting of his Mothers garden, turned left, walked around the balcony and opened the door to his room and gasped! It was his old room in every detail. He walked by each piece of furniture, touching, remembering.

The special quilt his mother had made him last year for his birthday covered the bed. Jane's painting of their special tree hung on the wall. He felt surrounded in love. Uncle Joseph had pieces of his parents' belongings throughout the house. "It will let us continue to feel their presence," he had told Jeremiah.

Yes, he was going to love his new home, he thought.

Hungry did too.

In the months that followed Jeremiah discovered many secrets of Talbot Hall. All the walls in the front rooms of the house were beautifully paneled in pecan wood. He had learned to appreciate the beauty of wood from his father. There was a secret passage in the wall from the front drawing room to the back of the house, exiting next to the back entrance. For Carsica's fast escapes, he imagined.

Jeremiah found he could push at certain points and a wall panel would open, revealing pockets and shelves. *Is this where Carsica hid his treasures,* he wondered. He found even certain planks in the pine wood floors could be removed to expose copper lined compartments. More hiding places! He was thrilled when in one of these he found a solid gold, hand held telescope. Even Uncle Joseph had not found the secret floor planks. How many other secrets would the house reveal?

Even the kitchen amazed him. Every kitchen he had seen was built as an extension to the house. This new one was *underneath* the house. Stairs just inside the back door went down to a huge room with floors and walls of brick. A large oven was built into the North wall of the room. The cook stove sat against the same wall. Plenty of wood was stacked in a woodbin to supply both. Window wells allowed plenty of sunlight through the eight small windows on the East wall. Four larger windows were on the West wall. Under the East windows was a water pump and table that held shiny water buckets and dippers. Oil lamps were plentiful when needed. A huge wooden table sat in the middle of the room with pots and pans hanging directly over it. Shelves on the walls held the staples for meals. A huge cabinet held all the serving necessities. Carsica spared no expense in building this lavish home.

Annie ran the house, but Maudy was queen of the kitchen! He had loved his Mothers cooking but some of the dishes Maudy produced were incredible! She fixed a hot drink he loved. He remembered when he ventured down to her kingdom about daybreak one morning, when he had been at Talbot Hall about a week. Maudy was stoking the fire for the oven. She was a rather tall, thin woman, with caramel skin, always wearing a colorful scarf tied around her head and waist.

Taking a sip from the mug she held, she scowled at him, saying nothing.

"Morning, Mam."

"Names not Mam. Told you its Maudy. If you want talk, call me Maudy."

"Sorry, ah, Maudy. Hanover is taking me hiking this morning. Is there a cold biscuit I could have and some of that coffee?"

"Yes for biscuit. Tis not coffee."

"Well I'll take the biscuit and could I have a mug of what you are drinking?"

She put a biscuit on a plate, sat it on the table with a jar of honey and the butter dish and sat the mug next to it.

He fixed his biscuit, picked up the mug and took a drink as he turned to go up the stairs, stopping, he turned and said, "Maudy, what is this!"

"You don't like, you don't drink," she said reaching for the mug.

"No! Maudy, this is delicious! I love it, but what is it?"

"Secret."

"What do you call it?"

"Don't."

"Well, I call it delicious. Do you fix it every morning?"

"Do not."

"Well, please let me know when you do. I'll be here!"

As he started up the stairs, Jeremiah thought he caught the hint of a smile on Maudy's face.

CHAPTER 6

Uncle Joseph gave him a beautiful white mare for Christmas. He was mesmerized watching her run in the pasture. With her high stepping, prancing, curved neck, flowing mane and tail; she seemed to be performing for him. Hanover was the one that cared for the horses and other animals. He spoke broken English with a brogue. He told Jeremiah he had been stolen away from his family when he was about eight years of age and forced to work on different ships for about ten years. Then about twenty years ago Carsica captured the ship he was on. He served on his ship years before being brought here where he helped collect clay from the nearby red cliffs, forming it into bricks and laying them to build this place he now calls Quanhoomas (my paradise home). Hanover was also the one that would teach him to ride and was a *wonderful* instructor. He was patient as he showed Jeremiah the fundamentals of horse care.

"Before crawl up on back, best let know who it is, and she goin to know you by how you takin care."

Jeremiah understood exactly. He daily fed, brushed, walked and talked to his horse. He learned to saddle, get on and off, how to balance himself as he rode around the pasture, and then came the day Hanover took him on his first trail ride. Eventually he became an avid rider. He would ride for hours through the woods, Hungry running beside, on and off the trails. He soon knew every crook and cranny for miles.

The Hathway family lived the closest. Seven boys in the family. Two were close to Jeremiahs age. John Robert and Thomas Edward (lovingly called TomTom by his family). They became fast friends the day Hanover took him on the first trail ride.

A younger brother had left the gate to the goat's pen open and Nanny was missing. They were worried because she was about due to deliver.

They heard a sound, something was coming towards them. What was it? Then...who was it? A red head on a white horse riding with Hanover!

Jeremiah was as surprised to see them, as they were to see him. Introductions were made and a lifelong friendship began.

Uncle Joseph saw to it that his nephew was not slack in his studies. He knew the importance of having a good education. He had enrolled him at Harvard and was determined Jeremiah would be ready for his August entry. Jeremiah was impressed by his Uncles' knowledge and Uncle Joseph was impressed by his nephew's quick mind.

He ached for his parent's but his uncle had filled a part of his heart with a new warmth that was comforting. New life. New ambitions. New desires. He had hoped to return to Edenton before leaving for school, but his uncle's busy schedule made it impossible. It was time to leave. How he would miss his new home. His new family.

His new friends.

CHAPTER 7

Pouring himself into his studies helped ease his homesickness and the loneliness he felt for Jane. Fueled with the desire to make his uncle proud he excelled to the top of his class. Time passed. Uncle Joseph tried to visit at least twice a year.

It had been five years since he had seen Jane, held her hand and heard her voice.

He read and reread her letters. He could *feel* the loneliness in her words. In a few months he would graduate. He would then begin a two-year apprenticeship with Oliver and Oliver in Philadelphia. After that, he would be ready to join Uncle Joseph's World Merchant's Company. Then he and Jane could marry. Begin their life together.

He had it all planned.

Graduation day arrived; he could see Uncle Joseph beaming with pride as he graduated…Summa Cum Laude. Uncle Joseph gave him some wonderful news,

"Jeremiah, before you go to Philadelphia we will spend the summer at Talbot Hall."

Wait a minute! Did I hear right? he thought. *He called me Jeremiah! For the first time in my life he called me by my name. Not boy! I have truly graduated!*

"And I thought we should take the time to stop in Edenton. That is, if you want," his uncle was saying.

"What are we waiting for?" he yelped.

They both laughed heartily!

He stood at the bow of the ship as it turned from the Albemarle into Edenton Bay. There was a twinge in his heart as they approached the dock.

Home. My old home. He headed straight for Jane's without slowing down. He passed people he was sure he knew, but there was only one he had eyes for. There it is.

Jane's house.

He knocked. Cinnamon opened the door. "Mercy is to me! Mr. Jeremiah is that truly you?"

He could not believe how happy he was to see Cinnamon. Just as he was hugging her, Darlin came rushing towards him. "It is for certain! It is him! You done turned into a man, Mr. Jeremiah!"

He gave her a hug and said, "Where is she?"

"Oh, Mr. Jeremiah, you don't know? They are in Williamsburg. They won't be back until Miss Jane's birthday. Oh, mercy me!"

He felt as if all his breath had left him. All the excitement of finally seeing Jane and now this let down.

"She didn't know I was coming. It was a surprise for the both of us. I guess I am the one with the surprise. Well, I *am* happy to see you two. Tell me about Jane, Darlin."

They walked into the kitchen and Darlin talked as Cinnamon fixed nut bread for Jeremiah. She sat the bread and butter in front of him saying, "Just like old times, Mr. Jeremiah."

Darlin talked for almost an hour, telling Jeremiah all she could about Jane. Her art. Her poetry. How she longed to see him. He walked out back, sat in the swing and wrote Jane a long, loving letter. He could almost feel her presence.

Leaving the Sullivan's he walked slowly and this time stopped to talk to everyone he knew. He headed towards his old home. He just wanted to see it. People were letting it and he would not disturb them. He just wanted to look. He stood in front. The swing and chairs were still in their place. Mother's flowers were blooming, but things would never be the same.

He found Uncle Joseph by the dock and told him the sad news about Jane.

"We can catch the tide out and go on to Talbot Hall now, if you like."

"Yes, I'd like that, Uncle Joseph. Let's go home."

Two wonderful months at Talbot Hall! He didn't waste a moment of his time. He romped a little with Hungry but he was not as rambunctious as he was just a few years ago.

Sheba was ready for him. Hanover had seen to that. Maudy had honey biscuits and his delicious drink ready for his early morning rides. He never told her when he was going. He'd pop in the kitchen and she'd have it ready. *How did that woman know,* he wondered.

The Hathway's were delighted to see him. John Robert and TomTom were home for the summer months also. So much had happened since that first year. The biggest was The Independence. A lot of time was spent hashing over what was happening in the country.

"John Robert, I wouldn't be surprised to see you in politics."

"That is where he is headed, Jeremiah," was the quick response from TomTom.

When Jeremiah wasn't riding, he caught up in his journals. He had started writing when he came to Talbot Hall and the tragedy of losing his parents was overwhelming. All his feelings were there. Uncle Joseph. Sheba. Talbot Hall. Jane.

Harvard. Everything.

He had not received a letter from Jane and now it was time to leave for Philadelphia.

CHAPTER 8

Philadelphia was a large city. So much to see and much to do. He thought he would like it. Oliver and Oliver was a thriving business. He took his responsibilities seriously and was respected among his colleagues for his abilities. He was eager to learn all he could about business and the management. Uncle Joseph was depending on him.

He didn't receive letters from Jane as often as he used to. Then again, being as busy as he was, he didn't write like he used to either. Surely she understood that. She should. He was working for their future.

I'll write her tomorrow, he thought. *I'm just too tired tonight. When was the last time I wrote? For certain I will write tomorrow.*

He socialized with new friends, had a nice apartment, loved the theater and went horseback riding as often as time allowed. In the almost two years he had been with the company he had been promoted twice. Unheard of before him! And now they had asked him to stay on! Quite an honor.

But that was not in the plan. Next week was his last week. Travel arrangements for his trip home had been made.

His friend Joshua had asked a question that had bothered him. "Jeremiah it has been seven years since you have seen Jane. How do you really know she wants to marry you? How do you know you still have the same feelings? How do you know she has not changed after all this time?"

He had never even considered that...until then. Is that why she didn't write as often? He felt a sickening nausea creep over him. He wrote her to meet him by their tree on May 6th at noon, if she still felt the same. He said if she weren't there he would understand. It had been a long time. He would still always love her. *But he would not understand! They had promised each other*, he thought as he ended the letter.

The Dolly Moorland entered Edenton Bay. The skiff took him to the dock. He felt weak, but walked quickly towards the courthouse.

"Please, please be there," he thought.

He saw the tree.

Jane was not there.

CHAPTER 9

He stopped. His heart was racing. *Where is she? She has to be here.* His very being had longed for this day. *She loves me…I know this*, he thought. *I will go directly to her house and ask why. I know I said I would understand, but I do not! What if something has happened to her? I must know.*

He was so engrossed in his thoughts, at first he did not hear his name being called. He turned to see Jane running towards him, calling his name over and over. She ran into his open arms and he enveloped her.

"Thank you, Dear God. This is as it should be," he whispered.

Wedding plans were made for the following Saturday morning at Saint Paul's. It was Jane's birthday, May 11th. Everything was in order. Mrs. Sullivan had worked many hours on Jane's wedding dress. Lovingly made of satin, lace, embedded with tiny pearls, it was exquisite. Since it had been an early, warm spring, Jane's bouquet was cut flowers from Jeremiah's Mother's garden.

The Sullivan's home and the church were decorated with magnolias, white satin and net bows. White candles burned. Jane rode to Saint Paul's in the family carriage, pulled by Nettie Mae, the family's trusted old mare. Even Nettie Mae had a spring in her step. Pure joy was in the air! They exchanged their vows before God, family and friends.

Invited guests enjoyed wedding cake and punch at the Sullivan's. Jane and Darlin's belongings were already aboard the Dolly Mooreland. Yes, Darlin was also going to Talbot Hall. Mr. Sullivan had seen to that! If that is where Jane was going…she was to go too!

They left that evening at high tide. Tears were shed. Hugs given. Promises of long letters made. They waved until they were out of sight. Their life together was beginning.

CHAPTER 10

It was a very uneventful sailing to the Eastern Shore. Jeremiah was relieved for his bride's sake. The skiff took them into the slew. They climbed the stairs. Jeremiah and Uncle Joseph beamed as Jane and Darlin oohed and ahhed when they reached the top.

Annie, Maudy, Hanover and his family were all standing in front of the house waiting to welcome the new Mistress of Talbot Hall.

They had not known about Darlin. While Jane was being shown the house, Hanover and his oldest son, Mikel, moved a bed into Annie and Maudy's cottage. Darlin didn't like this at all. She had been in calling distance of Jane forever. This would definitely take some getting use to. It would take some getting use to for Annie and Maudy also. They would have to share their home with a stranger.

Jane immediately fell in love with Talbot Hall. She had worried about being isolated, but she didn't feel that at all. She had responsibilities now. She was the mistress of Talbot Hall, and she took her job seriously.

Annie, Maudy and Trudie (Hanover's wife) loved her. Her genuine caring for her husband, his uncle and the entire family staff made that an easy task. They had decided Darlin was ok, too.

Life at Talbot Hall fell into a routine. Cleaning, washing,

gardening, sewing, cooking, canning, milking, making butter and cheese, gathering eggs, prayer time and an occasional visit with the Hathways.

The business kept Uncle Joseph and Jeremiah away for four months or longer but the homecomings were always joyous.

Two years passed quickly. Jeremiah and Uncle Joseph had been gone for five months. Everything had to be perfect for their return. Especially, *this* return.

From the time they walked into the house Jeremiah and Uncle Joseph knew something was going on. What though? The women constantly smiled and giggled.

Jane wanted to have tea on the porch. They sat and rocked, talked, had tea and muffins, then Jane picked up something from the basket next to her chair. It was knitting.

"What are you knitting"?

"A sweater," she answered.

"Ah, my Christmas present?" Uncle Joseph joked.

Jane smiled and said, "No, not this one."

"Good, then it is for me," Jeremiah said.

"No, not you either."

"Then who?"

"Either Evan Bartlett or Jessica Katelynn."

The rockers stopped. There was silence. Jane continued to knit, smiling. Uncle Joseph and Jeremiah looked at each other.

"What did you say? Who?"

"You heard me, Sir."

"That means...you mean...we are...you are..."

Jane started laughing and you could hear the laughter coming from inside.

Annie, Maudy and Darlin were standing as close to the open window as they could.

"Yes, my Dear Heart! We Are!"

Uncle Joseph and Jeremiah flew out of the rockers. Jeremiah fell on his knees hugged and kissed Jane, laughing and crying at the same time. Uncle Joseph, whooping and hollering jumping up and down, fell off the porch. Annie still standing inside by the window said, "Such actions. He hasn't acted the fool like that since he had too much of Hanover's brew eight years ago."

Jeremiah and Jane both quickly ran to help him.

"Are you alright?" He sat sprawled on the ground, smiling with tears rolling down his face and said, "*I'm going to be a Grandfather.*"

"Yes, you are, *Grandfather!*" Jane and Jeremiah both said, laughing.

Evan Bartlett Talbot was born November 1st, 1784. He was the prince of the family… a healthy, active baby, growing strong and tall. He became an accomplished rider, showed promise in fencing, loved hunting with his Father and Uncle Joseph, and excelled in his studies.

He knew the special secrets of Talbot Hall, loving the heritage of his family.

All too quickly time came for him to leave, as his Father did, for Harvard. Jane's eyes were red. He knew she had been crying, but what encouragement she gave him! *Mother might look like a fragile flower, but she has a stem of iron,* he thought. How he adored her!

Maudy had fixed a travel basket for him. "You a good boy, Evan. Your spirit will be missed here, but it again will return." She touched his arm and said, "A bit of magic awaits you there."

In the years since Jeremiah had joined Uncle Joseph as partner at World Merchants the business had thrived and now was one of the largest in the new world. So many times, they had talked of leaving the area because of the battles between Spain and Great Britain and the difficulty it caused their travels. They could afford to live anywhere they wanted but the outcome was always the same.

What they all wanted was to remain at Talbot Hall. So that was what they did.

Their hopes were destroyed in 1795 when the Treaty of San Lorenzo gave all of the area north of Mobile to the United States. Mobile remained with Spain. Uncle Joseph was older now and it was just too difficult for him to travel so he remained at Talbot Hall.

Jeremiah ran the business, alone. Evan followed in his Fathers footsteps, excelling in all areas of his education. Graduating, he joined his Father in business.

The following year he announced his engagement to Alexandra Anne Vendrix.

He had met Alexandra when she and her family visited her brother Adam at Harvard, who happened to be Evan's roommate and close friend. When he was introduced to Alexandra it seemed as if he were meeting an old friend again.

Immediately Maudy's words came to him…

"A bit of magic awaits you there…"

The wedding took place in Williamsburg, Virginia, on April 1, 1806. Evan and his bride moved into Talbot Hall. A wing addition on the East side of the house was completed in November.

Christmas was a special time at Talbot Hall. Jane had

always made it so. Green magnolia leaves with huge white and gold bows adorned the stairs, all the way up to the picture of Jeremiah's Mother's garden.

Holly and mistletoe over the doorways, extra large candles burned and delicious scents floated up from the kitchen. Jeremiah followed his nose. It was Christmas Eve and Maudy was working her magic. A white draped table set to the side, was covered with her specialties. His mug of "delicious" sat at his usual place.

"Maudy, are you ever going to tell me what this is."

"You already know."

"I do?"

"Sure, you know. You name it 'delicious.'"

He saw that hint of a smile he knew so well.

"OK, then tell me how you always know when I am coming."

"Ahhhh, 'tis my *magic* you want to know about."

"Maudy, you are wonderful. Thank you for all you do. Now you let Darlin and Missy help you, you hear me?"

He was worried about her. She still fussed at anyone who came into her domain, but her health was a concern. He had told her a few months back she was not a Spring chicken…and from her reaction, a mistake he would not make again.

Hanover had died seven years ago. Jeremiah missed his old friend and his gentle spirit. He had lived to see Darlin and his son, Mikel, marry and have a son and daughter; Kebo and Missy. Annie was gone and Hanover's daughter, Metilda, had taken her position.

When he went back upstairs, he joined Uncle Joseph in the front room.

"She is a good artist." he said.

Jeremiah nodded. He knew he was speaking of Jane. He was looking at her latest piece, a painting of Talbot Hall. The walls of the house were graced with her art. Portraits of Uncle Joseph, Jeremiah, Evan, Alexandra, Jeremiah's parents painted from memory, her parents, a self-portrait, many landscapes, flowers, Sheba, Darlin, Maudy, Annie and countless others stored away.

Dinner was festive and delicious and then it was time for the Christmas story.

Everyone in the household gathered for Jane to read her beautiful story of Jesus' birth.

At Talbot Hall, all was serene.

It was the last Christmas with their beloved Uncle Joseph. He died peacefully that night.

He was laid to rest with prayers and tender goodbyes, from Jeremiah and Jane, who he loved as his very own; Evan his precious Grandchild, Alexandra, Darlin, her family, Maudy, Metilda, the Hathaway's, Mathias, who came to live on the estate when Uncle Joseph retired, along with several other hands from the Dolly Moorland, friends and neighbors.

Uncle Joseph had designated the family resting area several years before. A beautiful spot shaded by three large oaks and surrounded with colorful flowers, facing West and the beautiful sunsets he loved.

CHAPTER 11

November 1814

It seemed there were constant uprisings. Not only was there war between Britain and the United States but also the Creek Indians. This dismayed the household. The Indians they knew were so friendly. Word came that there was a massacre at Fort Mims.

Jeremiah and Jane prayed their friends, the Hathways were safe. They had traveled to be with family and had not returned. Jeremiah and Evan's travels out of the area were at a standstill because of the unrest. They thanked God for their faithful, dependable employees that could handle affairs in their absence.

Alexandra announced the arrival of an heir, due to arrive in the spring. With that announcement and the news of the Hathways safe return and the news that the Indian war was over, Christmas was a time of thanksgiving.

The following February they received the joyous news they had prayed for! A treaty had been signed at Ghent between Britain and the United States. They were now part of the United States!

Peace at last.

Henry Colbert Talbot arrived May 29, 1815, a grandson to Jeremiah and Jane. Life at Talbot Hall continued in its usual routine. Jeremiah had sold all but 100 acres of land. More than enough for their needs or wants. The gardens flourished, chickens gave eggs, cows milk, trees produced fruit, there was plenty of meat, good water, good help, wonderful family, good health, and a very successful business…what more could anyone want?

Henry would tell them. He chose to go to school at William and Mary in Virginia rather than Harvard. Jeremiah and Evan were disappointed but agreed. He could have excelled but he found more pleasure in play than in studies. He barely graduated. Henry could be sweet and loving and at a split second, angry and hostile. More often critical than not and quick to see the fault of others but none of his own.

Jeremiah found pleasure in the memories of Henry's childhood, rather than this person that he had chosen to become. "If he had of gone to Harvard, they would of made a man out of him!" he stated.

"No, Father, it would not have made any difference. It is the times. He has too many modern ideas of what should be and doesn't have the sense to see his foolishness."

Nothing seemed right for Jeremiah anymore. His beloved Jane had passed away three lonely years earlier. She had not been feeling well for a few weeks. The doctor had said it was a "summer cold." Even Maudy's herbs did not seem to help. "I think just setting by the flower garden with their wonderful fragrance would be good medicine," she said.

Evan carried his Mother to her large, white wicker garden chair. Jeremiah sat with her. They talked and laughed about the "old days."

It is helping! He had thought. Smiling, she leaned towards

Jeremiah, touching his face and said, "You are my treasure, my darling. I have thanked God daily for you." Jeremiah kissed her hand.

She was and always had been his life energy. Maudy had sent Cinnamon out with lemonade and sweet cakes. It was a beautiful two hours.

"Time for your rest, Mother," Evan said, gently lifting and carrying her to the sunroom and her chaise lounge. Kissing her on the forehead and the tip of her nose, and covering her with her shawl, Evan smiled and said, "Rest well, my love."

Jeremiah sat on the porch watching the sea gulls flying over the bay. He drifted off to sleep, something he did a lot now.

"Jeremiah" he heard faintly. "Jeremiah," again he heard Jane and turned expecting to see her. Then he heard crying from inside. As he was rising from his chair, Evan opened the door. With tears running down his face, he put his arms around Jeremiah and said, "She's gone, Father. Mother is gone."

Jeremiah looked at him in disbelief, and said, "*No*, Son, she *just* called me. I must go see what she needs."

He had loved her for his entire life. Married to her for 53 years, and now she was gone. He was never the same.

Daily he walked through the house, looking at each piece of her art, touching it as if he would feel closer to her. For hours, he would set in the garden as they had that last day. The first two years he would not allow the usual Christmas celebration. It was just too painful.

Alexandra, whom he loved dearly, talked to him at great lengths as the third Christmas approached, telling him not only would it be honoring the birth of Christ, but Jane's memory as well.

He relented, but complained, "It just won't be the same. We don't even have the same smells from the kitchen."

Maudy, dear Maudy, was gone. He smiled as he thought about her handing him a red drawstring bag; with his name embroidered on it right after Thanksgiving.

She had told him not to open it then. "Wait for the morrow."

She did not wake up in the morning. She knew, he thought. She truly did have a touch of magic. It was the delicious recipe. Her treasure, passed to him. He placed it in the secret compartment of his Mothers box and put the box back in its hiding place, next to his huge collection of rocks Uncle Joseph had passed on to him. His journals were there also.

Everyone gathered. Alexandra played the piano and Cinnamon, Darlin's granddaughter, sang. It was a beautiful evening, full of remember when's and laughter. After the Christmas reading, which Alexandra did, he thanked her for her insistence. He walked to the front porch and sat in his rocker, as he and Jane had done so many times, and watched the sunset. Evan found him there. Quietly and gently he joined his beloved Jane.

CHAPTER 12

Henry had joined World Merchants. Evan kept him in menial positions, hoping he would mature and become the person he knew he could be. Unexpectedly he told his parents he was marrying Abigail Purdue, a socialite from Richmond, Virginia. He immediately set about telling them how they should talk, act, dress, and arrange the house and how the servants should conduct themselves.

That was it! He had gone too far. Evan told Henry to go into the library and he would join him shortly. He walked outside praying for the wisdom of words to use on his son. When he entered, he sat in Jeremiahs chair.

"Son, I love you dearly. It hurts me that your family is such a disappointment to you. You see, we love our lifestyle and since we are the ones that furnish it, it is not going to change. We do not have servants. The people in this household are members of the family. We take care of one another. I saw to it that you had an education. You chose not to use it properly, but as I said, that is what you chose. I have given you a position that merits your effort. Now, if you choose to remain at Talbot Hall it will be with the understanding that you will live as we do. If you choose not to, you have our blessing to make your own home wherever you choose."

There was silence. Henry rose and walked out of the room without a word. They did not hear from him for three years.

Although it was three years of heartache for Evan and Alexandra, not knowing where or how their son was, it was a life lesson for Henry. His socialite fiancée dropped him as soon as she found out he did not have his Father's money supporting him. His glorious ideas suddenly made his school colleagues go deaf. Without experience or the benefit of serious study in college, obtaining a job of position was impossible.

He wandered, living hand to mouth, eventually working in the cotton fields to support himself. He thought constantly of his parents and home and what his arrogance had cost. He couldn't begin to understand why he had acted as his did. He thought of his Fathers words. He thought of his superficial friends and the woman he thought he had wanted to spend his life with. Then he started to thank God for sparing him; he thanked him for opening his eyes about his life. He asked for forgiveness for being so prideful. If only his parents would forgive him. Inside his head, he heard "go home, *go home*."

He *went* home.

No one even saw him walk up the lane. He entered the back door, stopped and just took everything in. His Grandmothers paintings, the color of the rooms, the floors, the wood walls, the fragrance of the ever present flowers in vases throughout the house, the biscuit jar, Grandfather's chair.

It was such an overwhelming feeling. Home. Slowly he walked into the hallway. The clock struck eleven. He heard a door from upstairs open and shut. Alexandra started down the stairs. He did not move. She stopped, then slowly started down again, not taking her eyes off him. At the foot of the stairs she stopped and said softly, "Is it you or is this a vision?"

"It is me, Mother."

"Oh, dear God, thank you!" She threw her arms around

her son. They laughed and cried at the same time. Cinnamon and Star, her sister, both came running to see what was happening.

"It's Mr. Henry! He's come home…" and ran to spread the news.

It was a few hours later before Evan came home. Henry saw his Fathers carriage and did not wait for him to come into the house. He ran to meet him, crying, "Father, forgive me! I am sorry! Oh, I am *so* sorry!"

CHAPTER 13

It was clear to everyone Henry intended on being a Talbot and everything his heritage of honesty and hard work stood for. Having sold World Merchants two years ago and even though he had enough for ten lifetimes, Evan had opened a bank across the bay in Mobile.

"An idle mind is the devil's workshop." he could hear his Mother say.

Well respected and trusted, his bank flourished. Henry took the position of teller, determined that he was going to be an asset to his Father. That he was. The following two years he learned every aspect of banking. He was caring and dependable. People started to look at him as trustworthy, much like his Father.

At dinner, one evening, he was quiet for a long time, and then he asked, "Do you believe in love at first sight?"

He had met WilloMae Davenport and was totally smitten. The auburn haired beauty was visiting her Grandparents, the Hathaways. Not long after his question, there was a wedding announcement.

On August 4, 1843 at sunset, in the beautiful flower gardens of Talbot Hall, wedding vows were exchanged. The very next year a darling baby girl they named Deborah Ann, blessed the family. The following year another little darling, Kathlynn, joined the family. Girls in the family!

It was such a joy for Alexandra and Willo. A playhouse had to be built. Swings hung. Tea parties planned. Dolls made. The girls had their *own* ideas about fun.

All Deborah wanted to do was ride her horse, and she was becoming somewhat of an expert at only ten years old.

Kathlynn carried her little white puppy, Muffin, around like a doll, dressing her in doll's clothes, putting her to bed in the dolls crib, and even tried several times to let her have a seat at the dinner table. Grandmother put her foot down at that.

On August 22, 1853 a precious baby boy was born. A little redhead, just like his Great Grandfather. They named him Jeremiah David.

"If only Father could see him," Evan said.

"He does, Evan. He does," Alexandra whispered.

The girls adored their new baby brother. Deborah started making plans to give him riding lessons.

"Dear, heart, he has to learn to walk first," Willo said.

Jeremiah David did everything fast, *and his way.* When he was only about a year old, he managed to squeeze through a slightly open window and crawl out onto the back porch roof.

Cinnamon had cut flowers from the flower garden and saw him as she walked back towards the house. Running and screaming the flowers went flying wildly through the air.

Alexandra, Willo and the girls heard her, but couldn't understand what she was saying.

Willo went to the window to see what was happening and saw Jeremiah David. She had the presence of mind not to scream...raised the window slowly, and said, "Jeremiah, come to Mother," holding her arms out. Gleefully waving his arms, he toddled and took four steps towards his Mother. Close enough for Willo to grasp her baby and pull him in. Her knees went weak. She collapsed to the floor holding her baby, crying hysterically.

That was just the beginning. It was one adventure after another.

Just before he was walking well, Willo found him eating a sweet cake and reprimanded the girls for indulging him.

"But, Mother, we didn't!"

The next day the same thing happened. Alexandra said, "Jeremiah has not had his dinner and has a sweet cake in his hand."

Again Willo reprimanded the girls. They were in tears for being "falsely accused." The third time she found him with a sweet cake, she was in the house by herself. Alexandra had taken the girls to play with the Hathaway's children.

Not knowing what to think about it, she said, "Jeremiah, Mother wants a sweet cake. Will you give me one?"

He handed his to her and toddled to the kitchen, pushed a chair to the table that held Great Grandmother Maureen's biscuit jar, climbed up, removed the jar top, took out the sweet cake, replaced the top, got down, pushed the chair back into place, grinned and took a bite of his sweet cake. All Willo could do was shake her head in disbelief.

When he was five, Henry was astonished to discover that Jeremiah could harness his pony and hitch him to the cart by himself. And it was done right!

When he was six, Star arrived in the kitchen to find the cook stove lit and hot, Jeremiah David on a chair with the big black pan and a bowl of eggs, insisting he was going to cook breakfast for everyone. "What cha goin do, young man, is get out of my kitchen for I call your pappy and you feel the strap!" she told him.

"My pappy don't do strapping!"

"Well, he is goin start today!"

With that, he decided he better do as she said, jumped down off the chair and ran up the stairs.

He delighted in holding the baby pigs, playing with the biddies, milking their cow Bessie and grooming his Mothers treasured Cashmere goats. Of course there were pet squirrels and raccoons forever begging for handouts.

At age seven the family was traveling to Spanish Fort for Cousin Frances wedding. The girls and Willo sat in the back of the carriage while the "men," Henry and Jeremiah David, drove. The girls constantly giggled with excitement asking Willo all sort of questions about the ceremony, flowers, cake, and dress.

"Why do brides always have to wear white, Mother? Why not beautiful flower colors?"

"It is the custom to wear white as a symbol of the bride's virginity."

After the ceremony everyone was congratulating Frances and her new husband, Jack. There was much laughter, talking and music. Willo and Henry were congratulating the couple when Jeremiah David interrupted asking, "What you going to do with your goat dress now, Cousin Frances?" looking up at her.

"Goat dress?"

"Yes, that goat dress you are wearing now."

"Why, Jeremiah David, apologize to your cousin" Willo said embarrassingly.

"Well, Mother that's what you called it!" he said with a little frown.

"Jeremiah, I never!"

Others were now listening and Frances had a hurt look on her face. Quite loudly and now crying he said "Yes you did, Mother! Yes you did! You said she was wearing a white dress cause she was virgin just like Nanny goat and you always love getting Nannies virgin coat when they cut it off and you make something from it and I wanted her to give this goat dress to you cause it is already something!"

Big tears were rolling down his little cheeks. Everyone started to laugh when they heard his explanation, making him cry louder. Willo was on her knees with her arms around her sobbing little boy. Frances knelt down and whispered something in his ear.

He started to grin and wiped his tears.

"Remember," she said, "it's a secret."

He nodded. He was fine. Deborah and Kathlynn immediately wanted to know what she had whispered.

"Can't tell. It's a secret."

He smiled the rest of the afternoon. On the ride home the children slept. Henry quietly asked Willo if she knew what Frances had said.

"Yes. She told him that was the kindest thing she had ever heard, wanting her goat dress for his Mother, but it was just too special for her to give up and his big heart was the reason he was her very favorite cousin."

CHAPTER 14

When he and Lilbo were together, things happened. Lilbo was Darlin's great-grandson. His real name was Kebo, after his grandfather. When his sister called him, Little Kebo, as her parents did, it came out Lilbo. That became his name. *They were adventurers.*

When Jeremiah was ten, he decided to build a fort in the big oak close to the cliff, so they could see pirates approach.

"Well, I can see you need me to help, cause I'm a lot smarter." Lilbo said.

"What makes you think so," Jeremiah asked.

"Stands to reason to a *keen* mind like mine," Lilbo said. "I've lived longer so I know more. See, if you were smart you'd already know that."

Lilbo was just six months older.

Jeremiah looked at him and said, "Close your big mouth. All I see is white teeth glaring at me."

That made Lilbo all the happier.

"Everbody knows 'cept you, ain't no more pirates," Lilbo happily continued.

"Well, everybody knows '*cept* you that they are planning a return!"

The smile immediately left Lilbo's face.

"You sure?" he asked uncertainly.

"Anybody smart knows that for sure."

The huge oak was perfect for a secret fort. Three oaks had grown in a triangle and formed one huge tree. The full limbs made it impossible to see anyone or anything in the tree. The boys went to work on their fort. When it was completed, Jeremiah furnished it with a quilt, paper for drawing treasure maps, honey-biscuits, sneaked when Star was not looking, and the treasured telescope.

Jeremiah would disappear for hours and no one could find him. Evan scolded, he refused to give up the locality of his secret place. He finally decided he would trust Grandfather. After all, he understood about secrets. He was the one that had shown him all the secrets of Talbot Hall.

He enthusiastically told Grandfather everything....even about "borrowing" the telescope.

"Grandfather you must come see."

"I'd love to, Jeremiah David, but these old legs just don't work like they use too."

"Well, you can just set in the cart. I already have Jasper hitched up."

Evan could not turn down Jeremiah's eagerness to share his secret with him.

"OK, my boy. Hand me my cane."

Evan smiled at the seriousness of Jeremiah as he described the construction of his fort and his plans for its use. Evan told stories of the old days, and stories his father had told. Completely absorbed, they lost track of time but finally heard the worried calls of the others. They entered the house smiling but kept their secret to themselves.

It was a treasured day.

CHAPTER 15

March 1865

There was a lot of commotion in the home with whispering and talk behind closed doors. Henry had gathered the adults together in the library. The children strained to hear talk behind the closed door.

"The South is suffering tremendously in this war. Too many lives lost, property destroyed, crops ruined. You have seen how forlorn our troops look that has passed here. I had word that the Vendrix family was burned out. Frank was killed and the women, children and workers escaped by hiding in the trees. Now we have had news that the Yankees have come ashore at the mouth of Fish River and are marching towards Spanish Fort."

The women gasped. The workers shook their heads and Cinnamon started humming softly.

"This means they most likely will march past here and we have got to make preparations in the likely event they invade us."

They set about making plans about how to store their provisions, family treasures, (some priceless only to them), where to hide their livestock, where *they* could hide if necessary.

Henry was very concerned for his parents. Evan could hardly walk without assistance. He was afraid if they had to flee Talbot Hall it would be too much for him.

Alexandra amazed everyone with her endurance, but he still worried about how this was affecting her. Dear God, bring peace, he prayed.

With plans made, prayers said, everyone hurriedly left to do their jobs. The children were in the foyer and Henry could see their worried faces.

"Come in here, all of you, so we can talk."

"What is going on, Father? We are not babies. We need to know!" Deborah firmly stated.

If it were not such a serious time, Henry could have chuckled at her defiant attitude.

"You are right, but not one of you has been left out. I just wanted to make sure everything was understood by the adults before I made plans with my secret troops."

Secret troops!

They each stretched to stand a little taller. Henry proceeded to fill them in on what he felt they should know about the plans and gave them responsibilities of their own.

Every member of Talbot Hall was in one accord, *to protect their home*.

Two days later Crusel, Lilbo's father, came running towards the house loudly calling, "Mr. Henry! Mr. Henry!"

Henry heard him and ran towards the door.

"Mr. Henry, the Yankee troops are passing on the trail right now! *Right now*! Mr. Henry there is thousands of 'um!"

Henry, for the sake of all he was responsible for, tried to remain calm. He instructed Crusel to gather all the workers and bring them to the house. All prior plans had been completed and they were as ready as they could be. Food had been cooked and hid, preserves stored, paintings, books, and jewelry, all hid in secret places.

Talbot Hall was protecting her treasures.

"I feel like we are ready for a storm to hit us only it's a different kind of storm," Jeremiah stated.

"You are right, Son."

CHAPTER 16

There was a pounding on the door. Henry rose but Cinnamon said, "Mr. Henry, I think I best greet tha door. You understand, Sir?" Henry nodded and sat down. Cinnamon opened the back door, hand on hip, stood saying nothing.

"Where is your master?" the soldier asked. "The only master I have, Sir, is the Lord Jesus Christ and He is in heaven."

Sternly the soldier said, "*Woman*, where is the head of this house?"

"Mr. Evan Talbot is in the library, and if you are coming in *wipe* your nasty boots."

Opening the screen door, he and two armed troopers walked in, *without* wiping their boots, looking over the house as they walked through.

"What are all these people doing here?"

"We are all family, and family sticks together in time of need, and this sure is a time of need." Cinnamon said, and then asked coolly, "You have family, Sir?"

Without answering her he loudly said, "Evan Talbot!"

"Mr. Talbot is in the library and is not well. That door straight ahead," Cinnamon said pointing towards the library door.

As they entered, Evan softy said, "I am Evan Talbot. How can I help you?"

"Lieutenant Carmichael Henderson, United States 13th

Army Corps. We are scouting for provisions. We are in need of food, water and any medical supplies you have."

"The war has ravaged us all, Lieutenant." Evan was speaking slow and quietly.

"Our Confederate soldiers have taken all but our bare necessities."

"Sir, what supplies you have I must take."

"That will leave us with nothing, Lieutenant."

"As you said, Sir, it is war."

He turned towards Cinnamon saying, "Show us your kitchen."

Cinnamon looked towards Evan and he nodded to her. She showed the men the stairs to the kitchen. They emerged shortly with the bags they were carrying, filled with the little that purposely had been left out.

"Is there anything left for us?" Cinnamon asked.

They walked out, not speaking. She saw other Soldiers coming from the barn, and their houses in back with sacks. It was almost dark, but they did not light the lamps. Jeremiah and Lilbo had ran down to the kitchen almost immediately after the Yankees had left and had been giggling ever since.

"What have you two been up to?" Willo wanted to know.

"Oh, nothing, Mother."

"Jeremiah's done something, Mother, *I know he has*!" Kathlynn sang.

"Tell me. I won't tell." Deborah whispered.

Jeremiah and Lilbo just smiled and ran out the front door towards the bay, climbed up to the fort. In the lightness of the moon they watched the Union warships passing in the bay. They were scared.

"Ya think they ah goin *shoot us* if they find out?"

"They won't find out."

"Why ya think they wanta do this to us?"

"I don't know. They are Yankees. I guess that's what Yankees do."

"Ya think they e'va goin leave us alone?"

"Grandfather says wars end, so they'll go home. *Sometime*."

"Wish I could see them when they make coffee with that dried chicken poop in it," Jeremiah said.

"How bout when they put suga in tha coffee and start to pukka cause of that *nasty* pickle stuff in it."

They were laughing, rolling on the fort floor, tears running down their face. The boys in their own way had fought back on the intruders.

The war did end.

The Yankees won.

CHAPTER 17

March 2000

JJ (short for Jeri Jane) Talbot was running late. She was just going to have to slow down some. Thank goodness, her vacation was coming up. She had not taken one in three years and was so looking forward to a whole month off.

Working at the Metropolitan Museum of Art was her dream come true. She loved being a curator but it was her entire life. Her friends were co-workers inside the museum, no time for anyone outside, no social life, no boyfriend, no hobbies, and no family. She was going to be twenty-nine on March 5th and had decided to go in search of her roots.

Her Dad was killed in an auto accident when she was five. She just remembered bits and pieces of him. Her Mother, Marie, was reluctant to answer her questions. She thought maybe it just hurt too much. There were only two pictures of him in their home. Her parents' wedding picture and one of her on a pony with him walking beside her, a big smile on his face. She thought he was so handsome. She so badly wanted to know more. Her Mother's family had come to this country from Scotland. Marie, their only child, was born two years later. Marie's father had died before JJ was born and her Mother died when she was an infant. Marie said her father's parents were also dead and there were no brothers or sisters.

When her Mother died suddenly ten years ago she vowed she was going to the little town she was born in to find out what she could about her family.

"Hey, Girlfriend!" Corrine called to her as she walked through the office door.

They had worked in the same office for the entire seven years JJ had been with the museum. "Are you all packed?"

"You bet 'cha!" JJ said with a big grin. "Can't wait! The plane leaves at 8:25 in the morning."

"8:25? Whoa girl. You best get that pony in gear in the morning!"

"Yeah, I know. I'll make it."

Determined to leave by five, she didn't take a break and ate lunch on the run, and managed to leave at 6:30.

"Okay Girlfriend, call me from that little cow town you're going to and let me know if I have to send you anything," Corrine said teasing her. "You think there is phone service?"

"Yes, Smarty, there is. They even have a Holiday Inn."

"Well, you'll be out of the snow anyhow. Seriously, Little Girl, you be careful and please do keep in touch."

"I will."

JJ thought the world of Corrine. She was almost old enough to be her Mother and had taken her under her wing from the first day. She had never married and had dated the same guy for fifteen years. "Why ruin a good friendship," she laughed and said when JJ asked why they didn't marry.

The plane took off on schedule. JJ settled back, relaxed and immediately fell asleep. The plane landed at Dallas/Fort Worth waking her.

I wish I had a flight right into Mobile, she thought. *Just makes no sense flying to Dallas and then back to Mobile. Oh, well.*

It wasn't long before she was back in the air and landing in Mobile, Alabama.

She picked up her rental car and headed towards the eastern shore of Mobile Bay, her birthplace, Fairhope, Alabama.

Driving through Mobile, she promised herself to take the time to really explore this historic old city. *But first things first,* she thought.

How apropos, returning on March 5th, her birthday. She knew she was born in Fairhope at Thomas Hospital, but did not know where her parents had lived. "Well, at least I know where to start my research, she thought.   Holiday Inn was easy to find being right on the main highway running through Fairhope. She checked into the hotel, put her things in her room and immediately started to explore, stopping first at the desk to ask where to go to see the sights. The clerk directed her to "the museum, art center, downtown and make sure you go down the hill and see the pier and park."

Following the directions, she found "downtown," parked the car and started to walk. It was a beautiful little town. As she walked, almost everyone she passed greeted her with a smile, a hello, or even, "how are you today!" She was awed by all the specialty shops and everywhere she looked were flowers; beautiful, plentiful, colorful flowers in March! How wonderful! She had the warmest feeling.

This is my hometown, she thought. *I was born here. My Daddy is buried here somewhere, and I have to find him.*

Back in the car, she drove through town and down the hill towards the pier. She had researched Fairhope online and with its charming history. *A single tax colony.* She had never heard of the concept before. It just made this little town all the more unique, and now she was in the middle of it all and did not want to miss a sight or experience. She saw a little restaurant with a big "OPEN" sign, and pulled in. It was well past lunch and too early for dinner, so she was the only customer. The waiter-owner was very personable and answered all her questions about the area.

"How long are you going to be with us?"

"Well, I really don't know. I'm playing it by ear."

"How did you hear about our little town?"

"Actually, I was born here."

"Oh, so you have family here?"

"No, my father was killed and he had no family. My Mother returned to her hometown. I'm just searching for my roots."

"Yes, genealogy is a big thing now."

"Where is the local cemetery?"

He drew her a map and went back to the kitchen. JJ sat by the window eating her pie and slowly sipping her coffee, thinking.

"Bye, come back and see us," Carl called as she rose to leave.

"Oh, I will."

She headed for the cemetery. It wasn't large at all. There were very old graves and some recent, but there were no Talbot's. Puzzled, and feeling very tired, she went back to the hotel, took a long hot bath, and snuggled under the covers for a nap before dinner. When she woke and looked at the clock it was 6:22.

"Hmmm. I didn't sleep very long, but it sure did me good. I feel great and I'm starving!"

She took her time dressing. It was almost dark outside when she walked into the hotel lobby.

"Where is a good place to have dinner," she asked.

"Well, locally we have Italian, Mexican, Chinese, and country cooking. I like them all. We also have several fast food places."

She got directions to the Mexican restaurant.

"OK, thank you." JJ said turning to leave.

"You're welcome. Have a good morning!"

Morning? She said morning. Oh, good heaven's! No wonder I feel so good! She was laughing at herself as she got in her car to find a good place to have *breakfast.*

CHAPTER 18

She decided on just a quick breakfast at Hardy's and headed for the courthouse.

Not really knowing where to start, she walked into the license bureau. A lovely white haired woman offered to help her.

"I don't really know where to go to get the information I need. Perhaps you could direct me. I am a Talbot looking for any information of relatives that once lived here."

"Would that be Andrew and Louise Talbot?" she asked.

"I don't really know. I am researching."

"Well, Andrew and Louise live at Talbot Hall. They could tell you anything you want to know about the Talbot's. The family has been here since the late 1700s."

What? Talbot's are still here?

JJ's knees were weak, and she felt dizzy.

"Honey, are you alright. You are white as a sheet."

"I need to set down."

The woman, Arlene Prescott, helped her to a seat. "Can I call anyone for you, Sugar?"

"No, I'm fine. I just need to set for a minute. Ah, the Talbot's aren't in the phone book."

"Yes, I know. That's Andrew. He had the phone unlisted to keep the telemarketing varmints, as he calls them, from calling. I told him all he had to do was say; take me off your list. We go to church together. They really are great folks. I'll tell you where they live and you just drive in."

Arlene told her exactly how to get to Talbot Hall and offered to write the directions down. JJ didn't need her to. She held every word she said.

How can this be? Mother said there were no relatives.

She drove East on scenic 98 watching for the landmarks Arlene had given her. She slowed as she saw the huge trees and ivy covered stonewall with tall pillars on both sides of the driveway with an iron arch connecting them, proudly stating, Talbot.

JJ pulled in. She could not see a house.

The driveway was long and winding. It led to a beautiful two story brick and white wood home. The house faced the bay and the drive circled the house.

She slowed to take it all in. She could see beautiful flower gardens and what looked like grave monuments at a distance.

To the left of the drive was a unique greenhouse that looked like a little cottage. She could see a garage that looked like a barn, setting at the edge of the woods to her right and several men busy working.

She drove around to the front of the house. *What beautiful grounds.* She had a spooky "this is so familiar" feeling. She stopped in front and as she got out, someone called from the porch, "Hello there! Come join me!"

When she stood and turned, it was a lady setting in a white whicker swing. As JJ walked onto the porch the smile left the lady's face and she turned pale.

"Hello," JJ said. "I am sorry to bother you. I am hoping you can help me...*Mam*, are you alright?"

Tears had welled in the lady's eyes.

"*JJ? Is that you?*" the woman was saying very slowly. "*Can it really be you?*"

Stunned, JJ said, "Yes, I am JJ."

"Oh, dear God, oh dear God!" the woman was crying, with her hand outstretched towards JJ.

It was awkward. JJ didn't know what to do.

"*JJ, oh JJ,*" the woman kept repeating.

JJ walked over and sat next to the woman taking her trembling hand.

"Mam, should I call someone?"

"You found us! Oh, how I have prayed for this day!"

"*Andrew! Andrew!* Come quick!"

Within a few seconds, the front door opened and a man rushed out. He, too, stopped, looking shocked.

"It's *her*, Andrew. *It's JJ.*"

He almost fell in the chair next to him.

"This is so wonderful. I can't believe it! Who contacted you?" the man was asking.

"I don't know if this is a mistake or not, but…" JJ started to say.

"*Mistake?* How can it be a mistake? Are you JJ Talbot?"

"Yes, I am."

"Then it is no mistake. You are our Granddaughter."

Everything went black.

When JJ opened her eyes she was inside on the couch, and the lady was wiping her face with a cold cloth.

"Feel better, Honeygirl?"

Honeygirl. I *remember* that. She sat up and the man handed her a cup of tea.

"Drink this. You'll feel better."

"Thank you"

Slowly she took a sip of the tea.

"This is really good," she said. "Is it Chai?"

"No, it's Delicious."

"Yes, it is. I love Chai."

"No," he said with a chuckle, "it isn't Chai. It's a family recipe that has been in our family since the 1700s."

"I love it," and she took another sip.

"I really need to ask some questions."

"Of course, my dear. Ask." the woman said, stroking JJ's hair.

"I came to Fairhope looking for my roots. My Mother told me that I had no living relatives."

She saw the quick look between Andrew and Louise.

"I have vague memories of my Father and I wanted to see where he was buried. He wasn't in the local cemetery."

"No, my Dear. He is here in the family cemetery."

"Frank Talbot?"

"Yes, Honeygirl. Franklin Martin Talbot, your Father."

"Then, you *are* my Grandparents?" she asked very slowly, with quivering voice.

"Oh, yes! *Yes!* We are!"

JJ, Andrew and Louise were all hugging and crying when Minnie, the housekeeper, walked in.

"Land sakes and more! *What is* going on?"

"Oh, Minnie, it's JJ. She found us!"

"Lord have mercy, *it is* JJ! I would know that red hair anywhere! Welcome home baby girl! Now you all just sit and get all caught up! I'm going to fix lunch."

Minnie Washington was a striking black woman with snow-white hair. Her appearance belied her 74 years of age. She had been with the Talbot's you might as well say her lifetime. Until she started to school, she tagged along with her Mother, Darlin, (named after an ancestral grandmother) who *was* with the Talbot's her lifetime.

"I don't know what to call you," JJ said to her grandparents.

"Well, you called him Poppy and I was MawMaw."

"Poppy. MawMaw. *Yes*, that is who you are. I do seem to remember that."

CHAPTER 19

They began to talk. Questions were asked and answered. A whole new feeling came over JJ.

Belonging.

All three went to check JJ out of the Holiday Inn and put her where she belonged…at Talbot Hall. They showed her all the bedrooms so she would have her choice and she fell in love with the one that opened to the upstairs porch.

"This is adorable. It's like a ship's quarters."

"Yes, exactly. Your 7th Great Grandfather made this for his son Jeremiah. The one you were named after. It was your *Daddy's* bedroom. Settle in, and come down to the library. We'll continue our stories."

She put her things away and walked to the window, looking out over the bay. She had always loved trees. So few of them at home, she thought. She especially felt drawn to the huge old oak that stood by the edge of the yard overlooking the bay. She was smiling. *How wonderful this is*, she thought. *My family's yard.*

I have family. I have my roots.

She left her room and walked around the balcony that circled the downstairs foyer. She was mesmerized by the huge painting of a garden that hung at the top of the stairs. Other beautiful paintings were on every wall. She didn't recognize the artist and yet they warmed her heart.

"MawMaw, who is the artist of the paintings?"

"Do you like them?"

"Oh, yes, most definitely."

"Most were by your ancestral Grandmother Jane Talbot."

"Jane Talbot?"

"Yes. You are her namesake."

Art is my heritage. Imagine that, she thought. There was that warm feeling again.

The days flew by as JJ learned all about Talbot Hall. Poppy showed her the secret passage, the secret of the walls, the floors, told her the stories of war, of peace, of tough times, happy times and sad times, as he knew them. She heard the history of Jeremiah, Evan, Henry, Jeremiah II and on down to Poppy. From Jane, Alexandra, Willo, to MawMaw.

He told her of the family faithful…Darlin, Cinnamon, Maudy, Hanover on down to Minnie. He told how the old home had been so carefully "modernized" in the early 1900's and again in 1962.

Poppy was such a good historian. When he told her the story of Maudy, she took a cup of Delicious and walked all around where Maudy's kitchen had been. She could see it so clearly, as if she had been there.

Pointing to a painting, MawMaw said, "This is Cinnamon, and this is Darlin, Grandmother Jane's constant companion…" then they walked around the house and every painting she had admired was explained. Grandmother Jane had captured, in oil, those special members of Talbot Hall that she was now learning about.

Poppy had done such a great job telling their stories when

MawMaw said,

"This is Maudy, at work in her kitchen." JJ responded with, "Yes, that looks like her."

There were paintings in storage that she wanted to see, but they would have to wait for her next trip. It was all so much to take in at one time.

Poppy showed her some of the family journals. "Take time to read these, JJ. Do you journal?"

"Yes, but not seriously."

"Journal enough that your great grandchildren will know you."

To start with, he handed her a small, soft leather book with faint gold lettering, and a larger leather bound book.

"These were your Grandmother Jane's. After reading these, you will know her."

JJ walked to the porch, sat in the swing and started her journey through the journals. She could see the faint gold lettering of "Comfort Jane Talbot," on the front of the smaller thick one. Carefully turning the old yellow pages written as long as 220 years ago, the next few days she read about Edenton and her life there, Talbot Hall, her trials, her joys, sadness, her fears, her dreams, her passion for painting, her poetry. She read how she loved to sit here, on this very porch, with Jeremiah and little Evan during the evenings and watch the sunsets. How she loved working in the flower garden, and the greenhouse. Her life. It was all there.

The larger book was full of paintings and sketches. Notes were written that explained the page. *Hmm…* JJ thought. *This is very much like scrap booking today.* Turning a page she saw the very tree that she had admired by the edge of the yard. *I believe she sat here to paint it,* JJ thought.

Poppy was right. Now she felt she knew her Grandmother Jane.

How wonderful that I have MawMaw! Here and now!

She could sit *with* her on the porch and watch the sunsets. She could walk *with* her in the gardens. She could bake cookies *with* her in the kitchen. She treasured every moment with them both.

MawMaw asked her to go into the library. She wanted to show her something. As she watched, MawMaw pushed on a wall panel. It sprang open. She removed a box and sat it on the end table. Nothing about the house surprised JJ anymore!

"This was Grandmother Maureen's treasure box."

JJ could not believe her eyes. She had loved the story about the box but did not know it still existed. And here it was! She gently fingered the flowers that had been so lovingly carved.

MawMaw and Poppy talked a lot about the family's legacy. At first she had thought it meant monetary legacy… but that really wasn't it at all.

Legacy, she had decided, is what good of yourself you leave for your family to hold onto….of *values, faith*, direction and of *love* and determination. Like her ancestors holding onto this marvelous old mysterious home, through perilous times, lean times, for family they would never know, but *would* know them so well.

Like the treasured treasure box and all the *wonderful* journals, the marvelous paintings of Talbot life...and family traditions.

My legacy, she thought. *That* wealth cannot be bought.

"*Open it*, Honeygirl," MawMaw was saying.

Gingerly, as if it were eggshells, JJ opened it. She saw a

lock of hair tied with an old ribbon, a small tooth, a folded paper and a letter, both yellow with age. A faded red bag with Jeremiah Talbot embroidered on it.

With a look of astonishment she asked, "Is this Maudy's recipe?"

"Yes, it is."

She held it up to her heart, hugging it.

"Sweet Maudy" she said.

"We know there is a secret compartment but we have never figured out how to open it. I thought maybe you could try."

JJ did try, but she couldn't open it either.

"No, I can't, but I have the feeling when the time is right it will be opened."

CHAPTER 20

"MawMaw, I have to ask this. Do you know why my Mother lied to me about you and Poppy?"

"*Well*, for certain no. Marie was your Mother, Honeygirl and I would not hurt you by saying what I feel."

"*Please, MawMaw*, I have to know."

"*Well...* your Mother never liked Fairhope," Louise said slowly. "She was from New York and just could not adjust to small town life. She was drinking rather often and they argued quite a bit about it. Their last argument your Mother got in the car and started to leave. Your Daddy jumped in yelling for her to stop. She was in no condition to drive...

The police came about thirty minutes later and said there had been an accident. Your Daddy was killed but Marie didn't have a scratch. She stayed until the insurance paid, then she took you and left. I think she felt so guilty she *couldn't* stay. Anyhow, when we came home you were gone. We didn't even get to say goodbye."

"We tried for years to find you. We just prayed someday you would come back to us and you did."

JJ hugged her Grandmother and said, "Yes, I did."

JJ walked all around the yard, out by the tree, the cemetery, the flower gardens, all around the house looking at each painting, the foyer table and huge Grandfather clock, the library with all its secrets, the journals...the ones she had read and the ones she had not read yet. She sat on the porch in the rocker, smiling to herself, remembering Willo in her journal had described this as "just being."

She had to leave, a whole month had passed. *It just seemed so short.*

"MawMaw, Poppy... I am *so thankful* I found you. I don't want to leave but I have to, and I *will* be back next year."

"A whole year? Oh, that is a very long time. If you change your mind about the Mobile museum I'll put in a good word."

"Thanks Poppy, you're a sweetheart."

She hugged them tight and left. She could hardly see for the tears. At the end of the drive, she stopped, dried her eyes and headed for the airport.

"Well, the Southern Belle returns!"

"Hey, Corrine. Good to see you, too!"

"You certainly look like the southern air agreed with you."

"Yep, it did!"

"Hey, you even sound southern! Whoa, Pony!"

JJ threw herself back into work. She found herself leaving earlier than she use to. She started walking in the park, *even saying hello to strangers.* She kept two vases with fresh flowers in her apartment at all times.

Tonight she fixed herself a cup of Delicious and sat by the window as she did most evenings. Looking out she could see only cement buildings. She closed her eyes and envisioned the spreading lawn, the big oak, the bay, and the sun going down. She had always been alone but never lonely. Now she was lonely.

Her thoughts were usually of MawMaw and Poppy, the trees and flowers, their walks on the pier, lunch at Carl's, the sunsets, and church services at First Baptist. She thought of all the beautiful people she had learned about through family journals that had made her possible. She thought of their lives and what a beautiful story it was. And what about the journals she had not even read yet…what would she learn from them… and what about that wonderful old secretive house?

What secrets did it still hold?

Yes, it is a beautiful story…I'm a part of it! I'm going to live it! …and I'm going to tell it! she said to herself.

What a legacy Talbot Hall holds!

A legacy of roots and family values, dedication, heartache, and joy, struggles, success and *love*…! With tears rolling down her face, she picked up the phone and dialed…

hearing the voice she loved answer, she said, "Hello, MawMaw? It's me. JJ. I'm quitting my job! *I'm coming home* and I'm going to write our story!"

"Wonderful! Honeygirl! What are you going to write about?"

"About our legacy! The legacy of Talbot Hall!"

THE END.
or is it ??

TATE PUBLISHING & *Enterprises*

Tate Publishing is committed to excellence in the publishing industry. Our staff of highly trained professionals, including editors, graphic designers, and marketing personnel, work together to produce the very finest books available. The company reflects the philosophy established by the founders, based on Psalms 68:11,

"THE LORD GAVE THE WORD AND GREAT WAS THE COMPANY OF THOSE WHO PUBLISHED IT."

If you would like further information, please call
1.888.361.9473
or visit our website
www.tatepublishing.com

TATE PUBLISHING & *Enterprises*, LLC
127 E. Trade Center Terrace
Mustang, Oklahoma 73064 USA